T0283930

MOTHERLANDS

MOTHERLANDS

poems WEIJIA PAN

MAX RITVO POETRY PRIZE | SELECTED BY LOUISE GLÜCK

MILKWEED EDITIONS

(800) 520-6455
milkweed.org

Published 2024 by Milkweed Editions
Printed in Canada
Cover design by Mary Austin Speaker
Cover art by Yang Yongliang
Author photo by Ibrahim Badshah
24 25 26 27 28   5 4 3 2 1
First Edition

Library of Congress Cataloging-in-Publication Data

Names: Pan, Weijia, author.
Title: Motherlands : poems / Weijia Pan.
Description: First edition. | Minneapolis, Minnesota : Milkweed Editions, 2024. | Series: Max Ritvo poetry prize | Summary: "Winner of the 2023 Max Ritvo Poetry Prize, this engrossing debut interrogates history, identity, and the power of poetry to elucidate both"-- Provided by publisher.
Identifiers: LCCN 2023058927 (print) | LCCN 2023058928 (ebook) | ISBN 9781639551132 (hardcover) | ISBN 9781571317834 (ebook)
Subjects: LCGFT: Poetry.
Classification: LCC PS3616.A35788 M68 2024 (print) | LCC PS3616.A35788 (ebook) | DDC 811/.6--dc23/eng/20240125
LC record available at https://lccn.loc.gov/2023058927
LC ebook record available at https://lccn.loc.gov/2023058928

Milkweed Editions is committed to ecological stewardship. We strive to align our book production practices with this principle, and to reduce the impact of our operations in the environment. We are a member of the Green Press Initiative, a nonprofit coalition of publishers, manufacturers, and authors working to protect the world's endangered forests and conserve natural resources. *Motherlands* was printed on acid-free 100% postconsumer-waste paper by Friesens Corporation.

For my parents
鲍铮 & 潘晓民

CONTENTS

"When I am silent, I feel replete; as I open my mouth to speak,
I am conscious of emptiness."
—LU XUN, *WILD GRASS*

"But meanwhile time flies, flies irretrievably . . ."
—VIRGIL, *GEORGICS*

MOTHERLANDS

PEPPERED PATH

She walks the heady perfume of pepper-scented roads,
Strides through clumps of spikenard, scattering their fragrance.
—from "The Goddess of the Luo," by Cao Zhi (192–232)

they used to sprinkle the path
with pepper
so that it smelled good,
assuring.

that it was firm, straight
a good will. that no one
who ever trod on it
would walk awry. *a dream.*

it was good to dream
dreams in third-century
China, when bronze pigeons
floated around, literati
woke up to find food

on the table.
they smoked herbs
to get high.

now they use pepper
for a different purpose.
when we, the literati,
gather, they, the barbarians,
pepper us.

those pepper seeds, grown
in the warmth of South America
distilled—Capsaicin. *assassin.*

a peppered path: where
another pepper tree grows
solid, shielding
up the soul
from anti-riot vehicles.

二

POEM TO SURVIVE THE SUMMER

Ōe Kenzaburō wrote: *Summer—death by water.*
He was referring to the hot Tokyo nights, even the ducks

couldn't sleep. At morning, four Karamazovs rustle
in bed, thinking of money or the future of Russia.

Bach—a small creek in German. Circling back
to itself, like strings lengthening into willows

when I sit down at my piano. A nearby lake
smooths them back to say:

Hold on, my child, hold on. But the lake freezes
in winter and doesn't return my calls.

In summer I write. Two lines at a time, two vying souls
running up the wall.

At Runmarö, Tranströmer strikes a chord,
carrying Schubert into the blue of his cabin.

Summer is the time of revolutions: June 1966,
China was a sea of books. France followed.

In 1989, people were busy covering bullet holes
in Tiananmen, as Gorbachev ran back to his cracking union.

Summer sings the tune of birth and destruction:
Van Gogh died on a summer morning, the apples

of Auvers fumed with sweetness. Walter
Benjamin was a child of summer, but the Spanish

border smelled like rats and gunpowder.
Even Rimbaud, the youngest of them all,

squandered away his summer, his
amputated leg lying beside him.

When I think of summer, all the events
come to life like a childhood shadow play:

there's my father biking me to school,
my mother knitting in the sun, competing with God

to cover my limbs,
my great-grandfather, middle-aged,

spectacled, smiling like salt
etching away at the photo. He went missing

in summer 1949, his whereabouts
even the Red Guards couldn't figure out.

When I write about him, all the summers walk
in file. Then I lie awake,

knowing it is my time to rest,
like a child filling a bowl to the brim

with every expectation of getting more,
but an invisible hand grabs my shoulders

to say: Are you Weijia? Something's happened.
Come this way.

FIRST TIME TO A BATHHOUSE

In 1985, on the way to a bathhouse, Bà's head
was a gong eclipsing the sun. His ground-loving

flip-flops making a broken ragtime on the street.
Walking past. I was five. I had known

a few dangers. Those hot bāozi coming out of
a steamer, for example. Those fast bites

and a scorched mouth. Sān Kuài Qián.
Wŭ Kuài Qián. They were five cents

back then, dancing on my tiny fingers.
In the barbershop, I learned to close my eyes

when they washed my hair. *Let it go*, I hoped.
Leave one centimeter, Bà said. Then the barber

cut it all off. For whom
did I want my hair long? Certainly

not girls, for I hated them back then
for being different from me. How counter-

revolutionary it seemed to pee
while sitting. Walking past the bookstore

where I rummaged like a squirrel
for new comics, the owner chasing me away

with a feather duster: Mā never used a feather duster
but a towel cropped out of a shabby tee shirt.

You don't want the dust everywhere,
she said. And that's how I clean my room now,

glad I still have spare shabby tee shirts.
At the butcher's, an assortment of broken ducknecks

was a local cuisine we couldn't afford,
so we brought home some squishy stuff, still warm

from a pig, which Mā wok-fried with celery.
It tasted good

and was cheap, which was also good. As if
goodness is the same as saving up, as starving

ourselves; thin = good. Walking past.
A shop, crowded at the Spring Festival,

sold kids firecrackers; they exploded when
hurled at the ground. It sounded

dangerous. Use them up
before grown-ups confiscated them. Walking

past. A decent restaurant. A makeshift
chimney. A narrow doorway

to a half-lit staircase, where people lived upstairs,
inhaling smoke and dreaming from time

to time. Maybe about steam engines.
Every now and then, Bà would stop for an acquaintance—

Call Uncle!—while I would wait to morph into a dinosaur,
a policeman, a truck,

until I ran out of words, was reduced to a tedious
kid on the street. Thought everyone was bored

like me but they kept moving in different
paces and directions. We finally moved on, slipping

our shadows into a crowd's, while I gasped
for fresh air amid trousers and fists. Maybe

we had a real plan to visit somewhere, I thought,
like touring a castle or a graveyard of fighter jets.

So many secrets
outside my street that others must have discovered

and got bored with! But we descended the ramp
to the smell of soap and grown men's backs. To me

it was alluring: the rubbing of Bà's palms
against my armpits, my clogged ears for two days,

my penis that wrinkled and lengthened like a snail.
Should I tell Bà that an old man was staring at me,

long and long? But Bà's head lowered,
his wet voice ferried me there

like an offering. Then the man smiled,
his gold tooth a dark shine through the mist:

Yes I will take your son to my school.
Yes I will beat him and educate him.

MONOLOGUE ON AN ANONYMOUS ALLEY, 1998

At 7:30, an uncle wheeled out
a tin-clad trolley with
deep-fried rice cakes
which grannies picked up for breakfast.
The soap gurgling down the alley
is louder now; the neighbors
battering their clothes
say what sounds to me
like my language. Back then it was foreign
while Dad's teeth
clenched and unclenched
from work
or despair . . .
                    This was an alley
where fashion loitered
in the 1940s, colonial style
and the blooming patterns
on qípáo bullied
a kid like me,
a different
kind of bullying
from what they did to the "kid,"
aged forty, with cerebral palsy,
shouting up and down
the winding staircase.

I wish I had his perfect Shanghainese.
My teacher's spectacles
refracted blame
I was slow to understand.
I was reading
Das Kapital. For what?
The parasol trees,
shuffling tiles of lily

on overhead mahjong tables:
the gambling involved
little,
a grown-up's joy

in a world where I traded
my last toys
for adulthood,
the nameless store owner
shaking his head, as if
now, when I stand
in line, telling the customs
officer the purpose of my visit . . .

ÉTUDE EN DOUZE EXERCICES, S.136

*

In Liszt, I hear an old man stumbling across the fields to meet me.
He starves to save bits of bread for my pocket.

*

My own grandpa is different in a senior home in Shanghai:
He's polite. Asking about my age & name & marriage & age.

*

Time's time's timestamp. Which means that time keeps its own records
like a metronome, or a fountain blooming every twenty-five seconds

*

unlike the skyline that fades when the clouds loom large,
a flock of your imagination dropping on a book's dead pages.

*

In the early nineteenth century, Japanese samurai from the South
would gather every spring to discuss insurrection. *Now!* They would say,

*

finally: it was 1868, the Americans were banging on the door
& the last shōgun, a bony young man, would wisely concede.

*

Being an introvert, I concede everyday to my own messiness.
I read in my study. I love the fact that you're out there, reader.

*

But *glad you were not here* is not what a poet should tell another poet, as if
to imagine the world, we should only write about selfhood, the feather of birds

*

on parchment, & cold, thirteenth-century nights. How destructive
were Stalin's pencils, marking blue ✗s & ✓s on death warrants,

*

a color not visible when photographed?
He started off as a poet. A job I now have.

*

I remember another poet in Flushing, NY who told me
that I shouldn't let my poems end too easily, how I'd always

*

despised him a little, yet accepted when he rummaged for cash
& broken English, a fatherly way to say *stay alive* and *goodbye*.

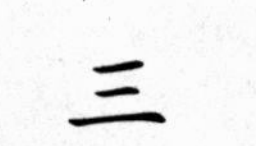

FEBRUARY: A DICTIONARY OF HISTORY, DRINKS, WAR, CULTURE, AND CORONAVIRUS

家乡：two tombstones on the same mound; hometown; *home is where the heart is* after death; the way memory emerges in horror at night when phosphorus fire flickers; tombstones are flintstones; those who refused to talk talk silently.

热水：as in a bath; as, when they dip you in water, Achilles, what fate will you carry on two slim poles; studying Goya's *He Can No Longer at the Age of Ninety-Eight*, I remember ordering for Grandpa; - *Hot water.* - *We can't do that.* - *Coffee, but no beans?*

冬季：a sojourn in Maine; pondering over the moon and my shadow, 3:12 a.m.; "We are now three" (cf. Li Bai); rereading Lu Xun's short tale about a date tree and a date tree; my printer is out of ink; embracing the cold for a jovial soul.

粮票：haven't seen these; back when coupons were needed for groceries grandma woke at 6 a.m., harboring them like a secret; cabbage sold out at 6:25 a.m.; winding this clock, you knew it would break; but when; she pedaled into her life.

黄酒：if I have this yellow wine, the sun will be redder tomorrow; have you seen snow falling from the eaves; a boy pocketing it, flake by flake, for homework; *have you seen a polar bear* he asks, pointing to his black cat; where did I lose this language?

诗歌：so I write poetry; truth is, I don't have a big brother who snapped my kite nor abusive parents; my pets grew to a ripe old age; I know every inch of my body is a danger to no one; I like history; my great-grandpa survived all the wars for me.

文革：you remember this as a color; the ground below is flimsy, but cleansed of blood clots; my family belonged to an unreliable class that wouldn't be admitted as Red Guards; Grandpa must have cried, an unrevolutionary act; where is he now?

新冠：*lit.* "New Crown"; a billion were crowned in China this year the gov't lost count; heaven's packed with royalties; my parents kept afloat, didn't get a knighthood; Mom scattered Grandma, who preferred sea burial.

记忆：every spring, cutting red paper, calligraphing the door; visiting relatives
to compare dumplings, jobs, children; much a-flourish; life moves on; the thing is,
I couldn't make it back to China; I built a shrine for my hometown; I live in that light.

MY OLD PROFESSOR ZOOMS ME DURING THE LOCKDOWN IN SHANGHAI, APRIL 2022

From 8000 miles away, even the most urgent sound
grows flaky and dim. He is old
in the graphics of snow.
He worries about the lockdown
and the residual hope in my fridge and rice bag.

"What is your reaction to this crisis?"
my old professor asks.
He pins the question on the paper
of my throat. *Say something.*
But too often I'm thrown back
to a dim-lit classroom, to the insects
I identified, the taxonomy of birds.

Many other questions in the world
he busies himself with. After retirement, however,
he starts calling his students.

He adjusts the camera once more
but still deflects its gaze.
Is that his grandkid toddling in the background?
She closes in, trips over the air,

hesitates, then cries.
Everything's a mess now.
For the first time,
I hear my professor cooing.

I remember
living at his house one summer, feeling
my nostrils soaked in the morning dew.
He made us congee. It cooled.
I mentioned the sound of crickets
he could no longer hear.

POÉTICA HISTÓRICA: OR, HOW TO LEAVE MY COUNTRY A VOICEMAIL

Now you're everywhere. I've known you for 50 years.
The fog on your face has lingered for 50 years.

No scrubber can clear up mysteries held so long.
In his room, Father wipes a mahogany box for 50 years.

That box came from Great-grandpa, gone in 1949.
He was an English major, a family tutor for 50 years,

until a patron made him a warden at No. 3 Suzhou Prison.
He didn't know fate would smile on him after 50 years.

Great-grandpa ran his little prison
like a laundromat. He tortured no communists with 50-year

sentences, nor did he follow the Kuomintang.
Great-grandpa was neutral politically. For 50 years,

he dealt with the SVO structure, practiced calligraphy
on old newspapers. This could go on for another 50 years

but that'd be unnecessarily naive, your officials said, hoping
to change a country, revolutionize it in 50 years.

They liberated a village, a city, a country, and from that country
to this tiny prison, they altered one-by-one those 50-year-

old, thus reactionary, traditions, replacing even the doorknobs.
Fired on the spot, Great-grandpa was again looking for jobs. In 1950

he went down south, and disappeared. An ailing man,
he left us a few photos, and the jawline that, 50 years

later, was claimed by my father. He closed the door on me
when I asked about Great-grandpa, as if saying *enough* after 50 years,

get back to school in America and *history should move on* . . .
I understood that. He looked for Great-grandpa for 50 years

and searched through the provincial archives, but couldn't find
even a death warrant, which would've allowed him to claim after 50 years

that Great-grandpa was a state enemy, that he was killed
for crimes he didn't commit. But you, towering over us for 50 years

like an iron cloud, raining down nothing: in 1992, you decided to liberalize.
Give us food, wine, and shopping malls. We'll forget your crimes in 50 years.

TO MY CLASSLESS MOTHERLAND

I bottle kerosene at a factory, sticking
labels with the firm hands you gave me.

> Dad had firm hands before he drank.
> He'd wake us up. A staggering shadow.

I woke up and left on Rice Planting Day
when Mom cried into a bowl of congee.

> When I make congee, I cry to myself.
> It's better when cooled, and served with pickles.

Pickles are cheap like a printed calendar:
the gods, festivals, Mandarin Chinese.

> Chinese is a weakling in a mega-city.
> The future is English, a tall white master.

At school, I was bright, tall, and pale.
I studied stolen novels under the dark.

> Dark is the color of small-town China.
> I bottle kerosene; I light up your sky.

ON THE RAILWAYS: A LITTLE SONG

Choo-choo, woo-woo, chooka-chooka. In 1885,
we build the rails. Cling-clang, cling-clang.
We breathe the steam at day,

we hammer nails into ties. Sizzle-sizzle.
The sun is high; our backs peel at night.

Cling-cling, clang-clang. Aiya-aiya. Our master
is a white man who plays cruel,
his eyes are blue. *You! You!* Whupah-whupah.

His anger a lingering red. At noon,
we rub ointment that smells like leaves
downriver. Cool-cool. Shhh-shhh.

His son has a toy train like a snake. Wo-wo.
Szzz-szzz. He rubs his voice
on our clean-shaved heads:

Ai'yah-ai'yah? Wo-wo.
Kueye'dien-kueye'dien?

His eyelashes so fine. His fingers embalmed
in white. *You come! You go!*
Yes-yes. Haode-haode.

He plays an old man from the sky,
he counts us like sheep. *One-two, three-four.*
The smell of bacon on his sleeves.

Our numbers dwindle. We came from different
provinces, but die the same.
Chinka-chinka. Chonga-chonga.

Whupah-whupah. Our master is thriving
between naps. He whips, he likes his rails.

He likes rails but not our blackened soles.
Dirty-dirty. Cling-clang. *Lazy-lazy.*
His shins are hairy and strong,

this bacon is not for you.
He kicks us in the ribs. Our pants are shabby,
hard work is all you need.

The sun dazzles. The boy is an angel from the sky,
he likes his growing train.
Faster-faster! Wo-wo.

Kueye'dien-kueye'dien!
Our master stomps with a whip he sweats

an era that must end. Aiya-aiya. Buddha-buddha.
The mountains are still but what do they know?
They stare at us.

Our ointment dwindles.
Buddha-buddha. Bodhisattva.
I want to write a letter for China.

It starts with the following words:
In 1885 . . . then the rest is blurred,
tapering along the riverbed.

THE PEASANTRY

The people, and the people alone, are the motive force of world history.
—Mao Zedong, "On Coalition Government"

I've found you more difficult to work with, which,
as I was told, is pretty much how you think of me.

I could smell the fertilizers on your skin.
You could smell the skinflint on my hands.

I could read history from the back of your reddened skull.
You could read me directly, reflected in the eyes of passers-by.

I eat porridge. You eat porridge. I apologize
to my guests for my lack of hospitality. You apologize

to tax collectors for the lack of produce. I think
I heard wars were waged to raise your standard of living.

You think "standard of living" is ludicrous.
I think even the communists betrayed you.

You agree, and go back to tilling your field.
I hate that your face is a mishmash of bones.

As a child, I pointed fingers at you.
When I went to see the beautiful countryside,

I admired and avoided you.
When I zoomed in on the rice paddies,

I feared you would emerge from them.
I feared you would blame me

for not thinking long enough of you.
Then I think *for* you. That's not that easy.

You prefer to think about cows and children
so your children don't have to think about cows and children.

But I always fall back to thinking about *you*
and you will have to learn to become *we*:

> When *we* finally organize ourselves,
> even the masters in the city will invite us to tea.

A MAN WRITES A GHAZAL, A SON GROWS UP, AND WHAT NOSTALGIA TELLS US

A man speaking Farsi for the first time in forty years is writing a ghazal.
He inundates his page with tears and half rhymes, a father

recollecting a pond where, many summers ago,
he lost his five-year-old son. When sorrow wakes him up,

who's going to stop him? Neglect is pain. A bucket's growling
emptiness by a dried-up well below a mountain is pain

stirred up by the wind. In Houston, my lower lip blisters.
Someone who tweets *no food* during the lockdown in Shanghai

is suddenly my friend. There's so much I can't say
in a gasp, as when a bird lifts off, or, when I push

an herbal pill through the foil, a chronic pain
arises in my stomach.

It asks me to call Bà and Mā, but searching
for ideograms on my mind's eroding tablet, I know

my speech is limited to this: that my life is colorful
because it really is worrisome, that another Asian gets killed

but it's far from where I live, the safest city on the planet.
I remember reading an Arthur Sze poem; a girl took out

her glass eye, and the boy who'd always loved her
knew that he'd see the world a little better, a little

more cruelly. Is lying a better form
of caring? Consider politics: a sea of lies

that my friends and I talked about all night
until the moon could no longer divide

the water and the mind, and I thought
of a border skirmish on TV

when the winning side announced *our retaliatory bullets*
entered their chests before their vengeful shells reached us

which was the best diplomatic retort
I'd ever seen from any regime. How imaginative.

How brazen. When a man writes a ghazal,
does nostalgia attack him first, or does he try to end

this civil war with himself?
He left his family for the US

so he could start anew, give himself another son,
a shady afternoon to plant all the daisies,

and forty years for his son to mature
and love him. I've watched this son again and again

in the stoutness of his thirties
pulling into his driveway, locking his car,

taking a deep breath before knocking on the door.
How amazing this is, again: a family, a house,

a street of leaves in a good neighborhood
that only whispers to him at night: *Go home!*

But he's sound asleep then, and doesn't know
I made him up for this poem.

WRITING WHEN THE WORLD'S A MESS

He was late for the flight.   She can't find her sandals.

He waved to her behind zigzagging stanchions.   She thinks

about her future.   He used a towel for the leaky toilet.

She scrubs the sink as rain overflows the street.

He hated continental breakfast.   She thinks *continent*, an adjective

for restraint.   He boiled water.   She weighs out tea for a mug.

He rolled up his sleeves while the TV roared *war in Kharkiv Kharkov*

or Odessa? No matter. He continued rolling.   She irons clothes

for her uncle.   He landed at a midnight airport and sneezed

at the stars.   She stays at home and becomes increasingly polite.

Later, he would check in at the hotel.   She opens the door of a drugstore.

He stooped down to answer self-explanatory questions

at the customs.   She peruses the cold eyes of her little town.

He toweled his hands before an interview.   She ties her pants

and stares at the pregnancy test.   He sneezed louder.

She thinks about her future.   He looked at a skinny girl

curling up on a poster with a donation hotline. *Call up?*

No.   She plucks the hair on her left chin and murmurs

it's عيد الفطر */* שַׁבָּת */* 清明 *and—does it matter?*

—unlocks her phone.   He felt like a chess piece.

She knows she's forgone.   He wondered if Fate worked

at the International Terminal in No Matter Airport.

She thinks the raging war makes no sense

because her hometown is already devastated.   He

tied and untied his shoes.   She tucks herself in

and the night comes falling. Her pulsing temple.

More than once, he regretted leaving.   She knows

as the rebels are near and the shutters are

heavy, that she'd better learn to sleep. Or not?

He was back at the ticket counter.   She reaches for her shawl.

He looked for his hometown among pixelated digits.

She latches the back door, thinking

how insecure she was when he first snuck in and out

and it was, what, five years ago? The rain stops. Dew

coalesces into held-up words. An incomplete act.

An unissued ticket. Wading through puddles

she feels her body heavier and when the pills congeal

in her belly, like two little eyes, she clenches her teeth.

REBIRTH

The night's drumming on tree trunks
with deepening cracks. On houses
bolted like cartons of truths. The grass
gives a low hum that stirs the branches
that hold a nest. A fledging heartbeat.
The fledgling is dead. Some boys
shot it down. They crouched weary-eyed
below the porch and when the sun
dimmed a little, their eyes widened.
Like a dead fish's. Like the full
tangerine, skin peeled off and curled
on my table. At night I stare
as if a hatchling will crawl out of it.
Clean it with water. Keep it warm
with my palm. Cup it like a child's face,
save for its narrow, blue veins.
When a life is kicked into being, it carries
the will to live and the cruelty
to destroy. The boys make slingshots,
wrapping rubber around the wooden Y.
The sparrows arrive with fresh worms
and twigs. The tangerine I nurture in my hands
will never hatch a bird. A bird
is a bird's masterpiece. A boy
is a king starting his kingdom.
His slingshot is modified with double
passion and when a decree is given
by the mind, the eyes and hands follow.
Now the sky is lacquered and the boys
have left. They were looking for the new target.
The skin of the fledgling they turned over
glared in the last streak of sun. A red spot
near the gutter. It darkens. The sky
grumbles, but will it cry?

THE MEANING OF CRAFT

"When they realized this," you said, "the rain
had stopped. The sun came out like an egg
and every droplet from the windows was
summoned. A car crawled back from a lonely

trip, which is not to say that the driver behind
the wheel had not gained anything, had not
found a snakeroot inside the bushes. But what
we know is limited. What we can do is often

woven together like a simple wish, so simple
that even its failure has a kind of minimalist
beauty, even its kill clause is—well, there is
no kill clause for it, just an indefinite waiting

for a response that might never come.
A test of certitude. Some would choose
to wait without an umbrella under the rain so
others would pity them, some would dream

loudly, then write letters to friends. Nobody
knows a graceful way to stop. So why are we
still dating? Why are you after me like a squirrel
for a nut? I'm not a tree. I don't have a tree's patience."

五

FOURTEEN INSTANCES

The flapping of leaves against a tree's thorny arms—

Branches of water on dissolving ice—

Magpies swivel into the drab sound of sparrows—

Along the bayou, a boy bicycles into a sip of spring—

Playing Chopin's "Ocean," your hands lead you to the sea—

One noon slowly replaces another, mixing up all the receipts—

How do you get by with a baguette in one hand and a pen in another—

Ideas chase each other, a succession of fallacies hoodwinked into lines—

At the end of the day, you work harder—

An army of ants escapes from the print of a typeset page—

When the curtains are drawn, insomnia wanders in a gentrified city—

Warming up, your thumb reaches for Hanon, your index Mozart—

Closing your eyes, you wonder if you're a shard in the eddy of time—

Life is a poem: you expect more when turning the page—

BETRAYAL: OR, WHEN A POET TRANSLATES ANOTHER POET

I walk fitfully into the moon of silence, aspirant.

~

The moon, fitfully, aspires to walk into my silence.

~

Silence my moon into the aspirant walk fitfully.

~

With fitfulness, the moon walks silently, and I.

~

Doubly fitful into me walks silence—the moon.

~

Triple the moon (mine?) in silence, to walk.

~

Walk silently, the moon fitfully to me, aspirant.

~

Aspiring to walk silently, I fitfully . . .

~

an aspirin silences fitfulness; I walk into the moon.

~

To me, the silent moon, in and of itself—

~

On the Path of Aspirants, a fitful silence walks over me.

~

The moon forks: all aspirants in frightful silence.

~

Two aspirant pieces (I'm their silence) walk fittingly—

~

FIVE CHINESE POETS

Li Bai

The moon
in a pond
on an ink slab

is the bed
where you bu-
ry your head

deep bet-
ween the
thighs of

a sonata & pop
up *oh god*
like a carp.

Du Fu

Split-second. Split
every-penny. Poetry

is a return letter
from a friend saying

no millet for you
that ends with

a huāyā, the joy
of a farmer's son

scattering seeds,
looking at you,

chanting *no millet no millet*
with the seeds still falling.

Wang Wei

of the Taiyuan Wang clan:
honor (horror?)
family (famine?)
displacement (displeasement?)

People flock
to your country villa
imagining deer.

Wang Changling shows up,
Meng Haoran shows up,
Li Bai's page
comes, bearing his apology.

Du Fu is a gaunt man
standing by the door.

The sound
of water dripping
on your stones
is edible (editable?)

or a drinking game. Now
everyone's drunk, you
return to your desk,
write a letter to Pound

before the geese lift off.

Han Yu

A bubbling wintry pot
In a besieged city, a wind
Two daughters sold for thirty coppers
As orchids wilt, a world of hatred
Cities built on top of ancient bones
In Chang'an, the court is a chess game
"I grant you a horse, a brush, and a dream"
Two prostitutes, waking to pee
A rescued city: an elephant foot, half-raised
Toothloss. Hairloss. Jobloss. *Das Schloss*
Philosophizing sarcasm in Buddhism
Early spring, then warmth
A new emperor: purple gowns, morning traffic
At home, measuring rice, no children
Unlidding, when the pot boils, a path
As orchids blue outside your study

Tao Yuanming

Thirteen Poems about the Classic of Mountains and Seas
is the title of a long poem by Tao Yuanming,
who lived outside of wars.

He lost pheasants every night
to the jackals.
Those jackals were government incarnate,
which he was battling,

according to some scholars.
He wrote about the Peach Blossom Spring
but never saw it.

The pheasants were lost day by day.

At thirty-eight, he sealed up his house
and lived naked inside

so he could be alone
with his imagery.

NOTES ON TWENTIETH-CENTURY MUSICIANS

Glenn Gould.

Glenn Gould is the pianist I loved when I was 15.

Glenn Gould had plenty of neck tension.

Weaving Chinese classics into discussions of modern sexuality and modes of representation is like watching Glenn Gould playing the *Goldberg Variations* while singing along. "Aria," "Variatio 1. a 1 Clav," then *Fire!*

Sviatoslav Richter
gay
companion: Nina Dorliak
soprano/caretaker

the boy grew up a little, unlike Horowitz
sequestered by a Russian ghost (depression)
on East 94th Street

the sound of water

the smell of anxiety in urine

"First, cut the lights."
—1938, KGB manual

outside: candies
scattering on the street,

unpotted azalea,
dark slush like cold coffee

no one drinks

ETERNITY

is the word when I stare at
a painting by de Chirico.
1913. Oil on canvas.
Anonymous donation.
A still life: then:
life. Crows
spattering down the pillars,
logs, spheres
lolling on the incline,
pondering.
And the sky: a bluish monotone
reddened by Castilian heat.
A hilltop city
with its own rules—
Where else did I see that
other than the slope
that I used to trudge up
when I was little?
But now, meters, sounds,
parenthesis, a bigger city
I must build
with the pencil of my body:
head down, feet up.

QUEEN OF CHICKEN

a chicken sinks
into the cutting board
outpouring
its insides

i think about
my grandma
about how she dislodged a chicken
for my lunch—
cutting it up
marrying it
with garlic and ginger
tossed into sizzling oil

surprising how little
i remember

only how
she squatted at the door

with what remained of it:
boiled head
soiled feet
a strip of skin

MOTHERHOOD

The scar of coffee
on a napkin
is a painting.

Beside my table
in a New York coffee shop,
a man talks

into his cellphone.
His Spanish,
almost indiscernible,

is beautiful.
But the woman across from him
is beautiful

in some other way.
Being older,
she expects attention

while sitting upright.
The sun dims.
The man talks

about a past of talking
and not responding,

while the woman counts
the buttons
on her coat.

On this day, you wouldn't expect much
from this world.

Someone talks into a
cellphone
and leaves,

someone stares into
the windows to
see herself more clearly.

When the first man walks up
to the counter,
the woman he's with looks up

with pain I can imagine,
shivers
and rests her stare on me

like reaching for a shore.
Later, the barista wipes their table
and they never return,

leaving me there
like a son, trying
to anchor the face

of my own mother.

READERLY DISQUIETUDE

*

When you wash gowns downstream,
a koi swims into a sleeve
from the eunuch's palace
several mountains above—

*

When reading an unknown language
hieroglyphically, a cloud
transforms into an owl
then a turtle upon a turtle—

*

When the wind stirs, a chrysalis
on the milkweed stem brews up
a giant idea about Zhuang Zi
through its cloistered ommatidia—

*

When speaking the wrong dialect
in a proud town, let
A become B and B become C
but C doesn't make D—

*

When you return to the scrolls
for inspiration, bookworms
have already written a polemic
between the footnotes—

*

When studying for the imperial
civil service exam, the unfathomable
depth of ancients is the leather
boots of an official who declares a republic—

PARENTS

A leaf falls silently
on a dead pond.
It misses the wind
tugging at its ears.

ULTIMATUM

If I forget one character a day,
I will have forgotten Chinese
by the end of 2042.

Sooner or later I will forget
my quarrel with my father,

I will forget if
I ever wrote to you.

And the new language
I will have acquired

will not be the same
as the one that bit me.

七

FACES

had my grandfather been an ex-guerrilla of the Malayan Communist Party

1

To get rid of acne, apply a pea-sized amount to your face,
rub, then rinse.

The pus
around a cut:

Don't scratch it, you thought.
In Borneo, you'd seen
worse wounds, itchy,
unscratched
on dead bodies.

You'd seen death:
counting heads after
each battle,
you scratched off the names
from your notebook,
every stroke
inching onto the page.

And your commissar,
squeezing his hat dry,
spoke:
It's fine, comrades!
There's still hope!
We are winning
by strategic retreat!

2

At night, the rainforest was silent.
The commissar
a snoring machine;
the sound of a creek
soared in your mouth.
You were hungry, and dreamed
of a soy bean, an adzuki—
luxuries
after enlistment,
replaced by slugs, or crickets.

You were eighteen, everything
was edible:
coconut leaves,
magnolias,
the latex
milky on your khakis.

The photo of someone's sister
in a crumpled family letter.
She was to get married,
he announced,
as if marriage
blotted out all questions.
And you, flustered, saddened,
walked
deeper into the woods
for a smoke.

3

What did it feel like,
married to an idea?
When you were fifteen,
your commissar,
whose regular job
was teacher of Chinese,
slipped revolutionary ideas
into the teaching of classics.

Where's the proletariat
during the regency
of Zhou and Zhao?
Why was Du Fu
a reactionary, and Bai Juyi
a social commentator?
He didn't teach you how
to read Mao,
his slogans obvious
in modern Chinese.

Soon you were
in after-class study groups.
It was 1963,
the insurgency was waning
calling for blood.
You snuck out at night
to enlist.
Receiving green khakis
from senior students,
you hoped to turn the tide,
save the Chinese
from the Malaysian puppet regime, and
the Malays
from the Malaysian puppet regime.

4

No. This is not a story
about revolutions,
not about girls
or the love of anti-imperialism.

After major defeats,
the headquarters were abandoned.
Your commissar,
whose hair grayed overnight,
no longer asked you
to grow a Marxist's balls of steel.
After major defeats
you abandoned your notebook—
hiding out would be hard
with secrets.

Then you were captured, but you
carried no radios
nor penicillin;
you knew nothing
about the "codebook,"
nothing about where-to,
what-for,
or who-against.
Maybe you were energetic
at first,
but they jeered
and strapped you down…
Did that explain
your scarred face?

5

After Mao's death,

you went back to China,

to the ancestral village

your grandfather abandoned

for a better living.

How does a nation face

its compatriots?

The villagers

put you to better use:

teaching first grade.

Did the students laugh

at your scarred face?

It was sweaty and glinting—

a joyful sadness,

chalk-stained,

clothed in a newfound

responsibility.

6

In this poem, I wonder
if I should even appear.
But you're gone anyways.

An old man,
you curled back
into your name, inked
on the lacquered
tablets, where older souls
towered over you:
among them, you
became a boy.

I feel confident
telling this story:
how you returned
when the camphor trees,
denser than ever,
cast shade on you.
Kids, in shabby clothes—
my aunts and uncles—
greeted you.
Then grown-ups emerged
from the dusty rooms,
with faces ruined by betel nut.
They brought you to the shrine
where they squatted,
flexing an accent
that sounded so loud, so tangible,
slipping through your fingers
like citizenship.

Everything restarted there:
the smell of soap beans,
of women drying their clothes,
of a brick stove
where porridge bubbled.
They stared at you for an entire afternoon
and gave you a broken bowl.

NOTES

"Peppered Path": The title, which comes from "The Goddess of the Luo," a prose poem by the third-century prince/poet Cao Zhi, refers to the old practice of sprinkling pepper on a newly paved road for good fortune.

"Poem to Survive the Summer": The title is borrowed from Robert Hass's poem "Songs to Survive the Summer." "Summer—death by water" refers to Ōe Kenzaburō's novel *Death by Water*. Stanza nine mentions two simultaneous events: Gorbachev's visit to China and the 1989 Tiananmen protest.

"Monologue on an Anonymous Alley, 1998": "Qípáo," also known as cheongsam, is a traditional Chinese dress for women. "Shanghainese" is a dialect mutually unintelligible with Mandarin.

"Étude en douze exercices, S.136": The title is borrowed from Franz Liszt's piano composition of the same name. Stanzas five and six refer to the Perry Expedition, which led to the end of the Tokugawa shogunate in Japan. Stanzas nine and ten reference Stalin's affinity for colored pencils and his early career as a poet in his native Georgian.

"February: A Dictionary of History, Drinks, War, Culture, and Coronavirus": Meanings of the Chinese characters: 家乡 ("hometown"), 热水 ("hot water"), 冬季 ("winter"), 粮票 ("grain coupon"), 黄酒 ("yellow wine"), 诗歌 ("poetry"), 文革 ("Cultural Revolution"), 新冠 ("COVID-19"), and 记忆 ("memory"). "We are now three" is from Li Bai's poem "Drinking Alone Under the Moon." "a date tree and a date tree" is from Lu Xun's prose poetry collection *Wild Grass*. "Coupons" refers to China's grain rationing system from 1955 to 1992.

"Poética Histórica: Or, How to Leave My Country a Voicemail": "in 1992, you decided to liberalize" alludes to Deng Xiaoping's southern tour in 1992.

"To My Classless Motherland" is after Jericho Brown's duplexes.

"On the Railways: A Little Song" is after Paul Celan's "Death Fugue" and Robert Pinsky's "Gulf Music."

"The Peasantry": The last stanza is based on a popular phrase in Mao Zedong's Little Red Book: "Revolution is not a dinner party."

"Writing When the World's a Mess": "عيد الفطر", "שַׁבָּת" and "清明" are Arabic, Hebrew, and Chinese terms for "Eid al-Fitr," "Shabbat," and "Qingming," respectively.

"Fourteen Instances" is after Arthur Sze's poem "Transpirations."

"Betrayal: Or, When a Poet Translates Another Poet" is a response to Eliot Weinberger's *Nineteen Ways of Looking at Wang Wei*.

"Li Bai": Adapted from Li Bai's poem "Quiet Night Thought" and the anecdote of his death by drowning.

"Du Fu" depicts Du Fu during his years of impoverishment. "huāyā" are stylized signatures used in East Asian cultures.

Terms, places, and characters in "Wang Wei": The "Taiyuan Wang clan," to which Wang Wei belonged, was a prominent political clan between the Han and Tang dynasties. "country villa" refers to Wang Wei's Wangchuan Villa on the outskirts of the Tang capital, Chang'an. Wang Changling and Meng Haoran were both Tang poets and friends of Wang Wei's. Li Bai and Du Fu were presumably not part of Wang Wei's circle.

"Han Yu": The line "In Chang'an, the court is a chess game" is taken from Du Fu's long poem "Autumn Meditations." "Philosophizing sarcasm in Buddhism" refers to Han Yu's animosity towards Buddhism.

"Tao Yuanming": "Peach Blossom Spring" borrows from the title of Tao Yuanming's story of the same name.

"Eternity": After Giorgio de Chirico's painting *The Evil Genius of a King*.

"Readerly Disquietude": The third stanza is a condensation of a tale in *Zhuang Zi*, in which Zhuangzi wonders if he is a man who dreams of being a butterfly, or a butterfly dreaming of being a man.

“Faces” is inspired by Ng Kim Chew’s stories about Malayan communism. “Zhou and Zhao”: co-regents during the 841–828 BC interregnum in the Western Zhou dynasty. “Bai Juyi” is a famous Tang poet. The staggered form is after Kevin Prufer’s.

ACKNOWLEDGMENTS

Thank you to the editors of the following journals, where many of the poems in this book appeared, often in earlier forms:

Action, Spectacle: "A Man Writes a Ghazal, a Son Grows Up, and What Nostalgia Tells Us" and "Rebirth"
AGNI: "Poem to Survive the Summer"
Boulevard: "The Meaning of Craft"
Cincinnati Review: "Writing When the World's a Mess"
Copper Nickel: "The Peasantry"
Frontier Poetry: "Betrayal: Or, When a Poet Translates Another Poet"
Georgia Review: "Faces" and "First Time to a Bathhouse"
Greensboro Review: "February: A Dictionary of History, Drinks, War, Culture, and Coronavirus"
Hampden-Sydney Poetry Review: "Fourteen Instances" and "Readerly Disquietude"
Huizache: "Eternity" and "Wang Wei"
New Ohio Review: "Étude en douze exercices, S.136"
Ninth Letter: "Motherhood"
Notre Dame Review: "Du Fu"
Palette Poetry: "On the Railways: A Little Song"
Pleiades: "Li Bai"
Plume Poetry: "Ultimatum"
Shenandoah: "Peppered Path"
The Journal: "To My Classless Motherland"

Thanks to *Palette Poetry* and *Poetry Daily* for reprinting "The Peasantry" and "First Time to a Bathhouse," respectively.

My endless gratitude to the late Louise Glück, who selected me for the Max Ritvo Poetry Prize and worked tirelessly with me during her final days. May you live happily among the Muses.

Deepest appreciation to Kevin Prufer and Erin Belieu, professors at the University of Houston, whose guidance and encouragement have sustained my passion for writing over the past three years. To Audrey Colombe, Nick Flynn, francine j. harris, Martha Serpas, and Roberto Tejada for support and invaluable insights on some of the poems.

Special thanks to Forrest Gander, Robert Hass, and Wayne Miller, whose mentorship and knowledge of world poetry has helped me become a better poet and translator. Hats off to Dana Levin and Arthur Sze, two of my blurbers, for their compliments and advice.

This book is also for my beloved friends at the University of Houston—way too many to mention, but here are just a few: Maha Abdelwahab, Ibrahim Badshah, Pritha Bhattacharyya, Rohan Chhetri, Lea Colchado-Joaquín, Rand Khalil, Iqra Raza, Kaitlin Rizzo, Will Seelen, and Adele Elise Williams. Kudos to Yaccaira Salvatierra and Vyxz Vasquez for friendship, proofreading, and last-minute suggestions. Thanks to my Chinese friends for phone calls, weekend trips, and discussions about the state of the world: Yingdi Chen, Ronghao Fang, Rae Qiao, Chengqi Wang, Tianli Wang, Qingyou Xia, Gaoshen Yuan, and so many more. I have benefited so much from your brilliance and warmth.

Much gratitude to the Creative Writing Program at the University of Houston, Inprint, the Monson Arts' residency, the Napa Valley Writer's Conference, Tin House, and the Virginia Center for the Creative Arts for their hospitality and gift of time.

I am also grateful to everyone at Milkweed Editions: Bailey Hutchinson for your meticulous editing; Mary Austin Speaker for your design and tireless search for the best cover. Thanks to Shannon Blackmer, Briana Gwin, Katie Hill, Morgan LaRocca, Madi McLaughlin, Daniel Slager, and the entire team for making this book a reality.

Finally, I want to thank my family: my parents, to whom this book is dedicated; my uncle for his encouragement; my grandparents for all the stories, told or untold. Thank you for watching over me and tolerating my mistakes. This book is for you and the world in which you grew up.

WEIJIA PAN is a poet and translator from Shanghai, China. His poems have appeared in *AGNI*, *Boulevard*, *Copper Nickel*, *Georgia Review*, *New Ohio Review*, *Ninth Letter*, *Poetry Daily*, and elsewhere. He received his MFA from the University of Houston, where he won the Paul Verlaine Prize in Poetry. He is currently a Stegner Fellow at Stanford University.

The seventh award of the
MAX RITVO POETRY PRIZE

is presented to

Weijia Pan

by

MILKWEED EDITIONS
and
THE ALAN B. SLIFKA FOUNDATION

Designed to honor the legacy of one of the most original poets to debut in recent years—and to reward outstanding poets for years to come—the Max Ritvo Poetry Prize awards $10,000 and publication by Milkweed Editions to the author of a debut collection of poems. The 2023 Max Ritvo Poetry Prize was judged by Louise Glück.

Milkweed Editions thanks the Alan B. Slifka Foundation and its president, Riva Ariella Ritvo-Slifka, for supporting the Max Ritvo Poetry Prize.

Founded as a nonprofit organization in 1980, Milkweed Editions is an independent publisher. Our mission is to identify, nurture, and publish transformative literature, and build an engaged community around it.

Milkweed Editions is based in Bdé Óta Othúŋwe (Minneapolis) within Mní Sota Makhóčhe, the traditional homeland of the Dakhóta people. Residing here since time immemorial, Dakhóta people still call Mní Sota Makhóčhe home, with four federally recognized Dakhóta nations and many more Dakhóta people residing in what is now the state of Minnesota. Due to continued legacies of colonization, genocide, and forced removal, generations of Dakhóta people remain disenfranchised from their traditional homeland. Presently, Mní Sota Makhóčhe has become a refuge and home for many Indigenous nations and peoples, including seven federally recognized Ojibwe nations. We humbly encourage our readers to reflect upon the historical legacies held in the lands they occupy.

milkweed.org

Milkweed Editions, an independent nonprofit literary publisher, gratefully acknowledges sustaining support from our board of directors, the McKnight Foundation, the National Endowment for the Arts, and many generous contributions from foundations, corporations, and thousands of individuals—our readers. This activity is made possible by the voters of Minnesota through a Minnesota State Arts Board Operating Support grant, thanks to a legislative appropriation from the arts and cultural heritage fund.

Interior design by Mary Austin Speaker
Typeset in Caslon
Adobe Caslon Pro was created by Carol Twombly for Adobe Systems in 1990. Her design was inspired by the family of typefaces cut by the celebrated engraver William Caslon I, whose family foundry served England with clean, elegant type from the early Enlightenment through the turn of the twentieth century.